Ready for Kindergarten, Stinky Face?

stinky face!

For Tuck and Kates, always my best teachers.
—L.M.

For all the new readers in kindergarten!
Keep practicing—books give you great adventures!
—C.M.

Text copyright © 2010 by Lisa McCourt.
Illustrations copyright © 2010 by Cyd Moore.

Library of Congress Cataloging-in-Publication Data
McCourt, Lisa.
Ready for kindergarten, Stinky Face? / by Lisa McCourt ; illustrated by Cyd Moore.
  p. cm.
Summary: A mother reassures her son when he imagines increasingly silly things that might go wrong on his first day of kindergarten.
ISBN 978-0-545-11518-6 (pbk. : alk. paper)
[1. Mother and child--Fiction. 2. Imagination--Fiction. 3. Kindergarten--Fiction. 4. Schools--Fiction.] I. Moore, Cyd, ill. II. Title.

PZ7.M47841445Re 2010
[E]--dc22   2009046625
        ISBN 978-0-545-11518-6

10 9 8 7 6 5 4 3 2 1   10 11 12 13/0

Printed in the U.S.A. 40 • First printing, July 2010

Ready for Kindergarten, Stinky Face?

by Lisa McCourt

illustrated by Cyd Moore

Cartwheel
·B·O·O·K·S·®

SCHOLASTIC INC.

New York   Toronto   London   Auckland

Sydney   Mexico City   New Delhi   Hong Kong

Today I start kindergarten.
But I have a question.

Mama, what will kindergarten be like?

Kindergarten is fantastic!
You'll love it.

But, Mama, what if the sink in my classroom pours grape juice instead of water?

That sure would be weird.
Washing your hands would be
a sticky job.

What if the teacher's rocking chair rocks
so fast it tosses her right across the
story-time mat onto the beanbag chair?

I bet you'd be the next to try it!

I would!
But, Mama, what if the fish tank
starts to grow, and it gets as big
as the whole classroom?

I'd put a swimsuit in your backpack, just in case.

What if a hungry armadillo chases me at art time to eat my macaroni necklace?

Just give it to him.
You can always make another one.

But, Mama, the sink will probably pour water, right?

Probably.

And probably the chairs and the fish tank and art class will be regular.

Probably.
But there is *one* wonderfully silly thing
I know will be at your new school.

I know, Mama.